Girl, You Are Awesome!

Inspiring Short Stories About Confidence,
Courage, Perseverance and Friendship

Avia Joyce

Thank you for buying our book!

If you find this storybook fun and useful, we would be very grateful if you could post a short review on Amazon! Your support does make a difference and we read every review personally.

If you would like to leave a review, just head on over to this book's Amazon page and click "Write a customer review."

Thank you for your support!

Table of Contents

Jumping for Joy!

"Found another one!" Harper exclaimed as she dived for the colorful egg hidden underneath a bush.

Her tanned face flushed with the excitement that was building up inside of her. This was her favorite part of Easter—the egg hunt in the local park.

Her friends all moved on around her, searching for the next egg. They each wanted to be the one who got the most eggs. Every time Harper looked around, her friends all rushed by in colorful blurs.

But Harper wasn't in a hurry. She didn't want to have the most eggs. No, Harper wanted to find the *best* Easter egg of the year!

Bending down low to the ground, the little girl searched for any hidden treasures. *You don't find the best ones easily*, Harper thought when she spotted another one hiding in a hedge nearby.

She crawled on her belly, still holding onto the basket with the rest of her eggs. Her curly black hair got

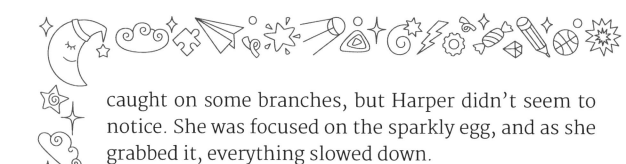

caught on some branches, but Harper didn't seem to notice. She was focused on the sparkly egg, and as she grabbed it, everything slowed down.

Harper crawled back out of the hedge with the egg in her tiny hand and wondered what had happened. *Why is everyone moving so slowly?*

She looked at her friends, Claire and Nelly. They were both dashing for the same place but moving as slow as turtles. She then tried to find her mom and little brother, but they were also stuck in slow-motion.

Just then, a jumping white spot caught her eye. Harper tried to look at what it was, but it was near the edge of the forest. The forest was on the other side of the park!

Harper ran across the park and toward the white flash. With everyone moving slowly, she felt like she was running super fast! Her basket hit her leg with every step she took, and Harper tightened her hand around the sparkly egg.

The closer she came to the forest, the easier it was for her to see what the jumping white flash was. *It's a bunny!*

But this wasn't any ordinary bunny. When Harper finally ran all the way to it, she saw that this bunny was big and white and wore a blue striped shirt with a little red tie. He had a pink belly and a pink nose. His whiskers were long and black, and his huge feet were helping him to bounce really high! Higher than Harper ever could!

"Hello," she said, looking at the bunny with wide eyes.

"There you are! I've been waiting *all* day for you, Harper!" The bunny kept bouncing and bouncing with a huge smile on his face.

"You have? But I don't know you."

"Of course you do!" *Bounce bounce bounce* he went. Harper felt dizzy from looking at it.

"I've never seen you before."

Finally, the bunny stopped jumping and looked at Harper. "Well, where did you get all of those fancy eggs you have in your basket there?"

"From the Easter Bunny."

"Right! So you do know who I am!"

"You're... the Easter Bunny?" Harper was excited again. No one had ever seen the Easter Bunny, and now he was right in front of her.

"Yes, I am. Pleased to meet you, Harper." He bowed to her.

"You too, Mr. Easter Bunny! But what are you doing here?" Harper sat down on the grass where she was standing, and the bunny joined her.

"I'm here to help you find the best egg of all! Isn't that what you wanted?"

"Yes! Yes! Yes!"

"Good! Then follow me!" Harper watched as the Easter Bunny got up and hopped into the forest.

She really wanted to follow him, but the forest looked scary up close. Harper looked back at her friends and family—they were still in slow-motion.

"Come on, Harper!" She heard him call and went to find him in the forest. *You can do this, Harper. Nothing's going to hurt you.*

She saw him waiting for her by a giant tree, a big smile on his face. It made her feel safe now and ready to find the best egg.

"I'm ready, Mr. Easter Bunny!"

"Hop with me!" The Easter Bunny bounced through the forest with Harper hopping along behind him.

She saw so many animals as they went deeper and deeper. There were two birds. One was as red as the candy apple her mom gave her earlier and the other as blue as the sky. They whistled when Harper and the bunny passed them.

When Harper looked back to see how far they had gone, she saw the two birds flying along with her. They weren't the only ones that joined them. There was a little squirrel and a chubby chipmunk. A black badger and a running raccoon.

She even saw some deer prance along next to them! Harper loved being surrounded by the animals and no longer thought of the forest as a scary place.

Then she hit something hard in front of her and fell to the ground, her basket of eggs rolling away from her.

"My eggs!" she cried. Harper crawled after it and grabbed it before the eggs fell out.

Looking up to see what she'd hit, she saw the Easter Bunny smiling down at her. "Sorry about that, Harper. Seemed like you weren't looking where you were going."

He laughed and held out his paw. Harper took it, letting the bunny pull her up, and that's when she saw it.

Behind him, an egg the size of a football glowed in the warm sun. *Wow!* Harper thought as she walked to it.

"It's so big! And golden!"

"And it's yours, Harper."

"Are you sure?" She turned and looked at the Easter Bunny.

"Very! I made this egg especially for you. It's a special egg and when you go back to the park, I want you to crack it open for a surprise!"

The Easter Bunny was now jumping with even more excitement. Harper gently picked up the golden egg, making sure to keep it safe.

"Thank you so much, Mr. Easter Bunny!"

"You're welcome, Harper. You're a very special girl. Every year, you don't race to get the most eggs. You look for the ones nobody else finds. Easter isn't about finding the most eggs. It's about finding the magic hidden away. Come now, let's get back to your friends and family!"

Harper smiled at the bunny as he turned and started hopping back the way they came. Tired from all the bouncing earlier and also not wanting to break the egg, Harper quickly walked back to the edge of the forest.

She saw everyone still racing in slow moves and turned back to the Easter Bunny. "Are they going to be alright?"

"Of course!" With a snap of his fingers, everyone started moving normally again. "Go on, Harper. Have a happy Easter!"

"You too, Mr. Easter Bunny!" She started running back across the park and yelled to him, "Thank you again!"

Harper ran as fast as her little legs could take her, keeping the golden egg close in her arms.

"Look! Everyone, look what I found!" she shouted when she got near enough. All her friends and family looked to see Harper holding up the giant egg and quickly came running to her.

"Wow! Where did you find *that*?" her little brother asked.

"The Easter Bunny helped me find it."

"You saw the Easter Bunny?" her friend Claire exclaimed.

"Yeah! It was so much fun!" Everyone started talking and looking at the egg, but Harper looked behind her at the forest.

She could just see the movement of something white before it disappeared into the trees. Smiling, she remembered what the Easter Bunny had asked her to do.

"Everyone, step back! There's a surprise!" They were all so eager to see the surprise that they listened to what Harper said.

She called her little brother to come closer, handing him the egg. "The Easter Bunny said to crack it open and I want you to do it."

Her brother smiled up at her before dropping the egg hard onto the ground, cracking it open. Out came the most beautiful rainbow that Harper had ever seen!

The colors were so bright and wonderful in the clear blue sky. Red, orange, yellow, green, blue, indigo, and

violet—all shining just as bright as the golden egg was!

"Wow!" all the people shouted, looking at the magic right above them.

"Happy Easter!" someone shouted.

"Happy Easter!" everyone said.

Harper spent the rest of the day playing with her little brother and friends. The rainbow stayed in the sky the whole day and made everyone smile when they saw it. They had a big lunch in the park and everyone showed off the eggs that they found, but best of all, everyone talked about the amazing egg of Harper's!

Harper couldn't stop thinking about what the Easter Bunny had given her. She made a promise to try to do something as nice as that to someone each Easter.

The Easter Bunny said she was special. *What made Easter really special was making each other happy,* Harper thought as she looked up at the rainbow smiling down upon them all.

Believing in Magic

"Come, one and come, all. Just one breath. That is my call. Your wishes aren't small. Let them fall!"

"Fall from what?" Ella paused at the strange lady's booth. Her parents walked on to the next one.

The lady with fiery red hair and emerald eyes smiled down at Ella. "Well, your lips, my dear. How else do you make a wish?"

"I don't believe in wishes," Ella whispered.

A wind blew across the courtyard where the festival had been set up. Many people had come from all over the country to share their objects and gifts.

Ella didn't want to come when her parents told her about it. She was 13 now and didn't *need* to go everywhere with them. But they made her come anyway, promising ice-cream afterwards.

"My dear, what do you mean you don't believe in wishes? Wishes are powerful," the lady said to her.

Ella shrugged her shoulders and looked behind the

woman at what she was selling. "Are those candles?"

"They are indeed." The older lady looked down at Ella once more before she said, Let me show you how to make one. I think you'd really like it."

"Okay. Let me ask my mom and dad." Ella walked to her parents and asked if she could make a candle.

Her mom smiled at her and said she knew that Ella would find something she liked at the festival. The blond girl ran back to the candle booth and found the lady had been waiting for her.

"Come, child, let us begin."

"I'm not a child. My name's Ella," she said and stood next to the woman.

"Ah, I see. Okay then, *Ella*, you can call me Ivy." Ivy gave Ella a smile that made her feel all light and airy inside.

She shook it off and reached for the small candle that Ivy held out to her. "But this candle has already been made."

"Not completely. You see, I used a special wax for the inside of your candle."

"A special wax? What for?" Ella asked when she looked at the tiny thing in her hand.

"Well, it's sort of like people. Who we are on the inside is what really matters. Don't you think so?" Ivy asked.

"I guess." Ella shrugged again and thought the lady was really strange.

Ivy called Ella to follow her to the other side of the booth where various cans had been set up. There were different colors in each can and Ella saw that it was wax.

"So how does this work?" Ella asked.

"You take the candle I gave you and you dip it into a can with whichever color you want. Then you dip it into the cold water to harden it and repeat the process, either with the same color or a different one."

"But if you use different colors, how will you see them?"

"Good question!" Ivy pointed to another table. "Once your candle is made, we will craft it into a design that matches you."

Ella looked at Ivy, confused. "I don't understand. How can you do that?"

"By using magic!" Ivy wiggled her fingers, and something that looked like glitter fell out of them. Ella knew that she was playing a trick on her and that glitter hadn't really come out of her fingertips.

"If you say so."

"Ella, you don't believe in wishes or magic?" Ivy looked at her with a sad smile.

"I don't think I do. I'd like to make my candle now."

"Alright, dear, come over here." Ella walked to Ivy and the cans of colors. She was about to dip the candle in the first can when Ivy stopped her.

"It's important that you choose which colors you want to use."

"Why?"

"Because of the magic! It helps you when you don't

think you need it." Ella saw Ivy smile and thought about what she said.

"Okay… Then I want to do green."

"Green is for nature. It shows your love for it and being surrounded by it."

Ella was drawn to that first color and dipped her candle in it. She then put it in the water like Ivy said and dipped it two more times in the green. Ivy told Ella that by doing each color three times, it would make her candle even more magical.

"And blue?"

"That is for strength. Strength to be who you are and to help others."

Again, Ella felt drawn to the blue and dipped her candle in it three times. "Purple?"

"That is for imagination. I particularly like this color as it helps me see things I normally wouldn't."

Ella had become fascinated by the meanings and the wonder of what Ivy was telling her. She dipped her candle in the purple then repeated the colors—green, blue, and purple. Then she did it one last time before looking back at Ivy.

The older woman had a small smile on her face, and Ivy felt embarrassed. "I'm sorry. I didn't mean to take up so much of your wax."

"Never worry about that, my dear. There will always be more. Come, let us seal your candle with the purity of white."

"Why white?" Ella asked as she followed Ivy to the last can and dipped it in three times.

"White helps to protect the innocent, like you and your candle. It is interesting that you were drawn to the cool colors."

"I don't know. It just felt… right. And I like those colors the most!" Ella smiled at Ivy.

"They are pretty amazing, aren't they? Green, blue, and purple. Do you know what they mean all together?" Ivy hung the candle up to dry for a bit, and Ella helped her clean up.

She looked around and saw her parents at another booth across the way. Ella shook her head and waited for Ivy to tell her.

"They mean love, peace, wisdom, and creativity."

Ella was finally understanding the importance of

the colors. It was about her and what she found most important.

"That is so cool!"

"It really is, Ella. Can I ask you again why you don't believe in magic and wishes?"

Ella looked at the floor. "My aunt is sick, and she hasn't gotten better, no matter how much I wish she would."

"Oh, Ella, I'm so sorry. Let me see if I can help."

Ella watched as Ivy took her candle down and then followed her to the table. "How can you help?"

"Remember, I told you I will carve your candle into a design that matches you?" Ella nodded her head. "Before I do that, I want you to blow on the candle with everything you have, okay?"

Ivy handed her the candle, and Ella sucked in a deep breath. She blew it out on the candle as best as she could. She gave it back to a smiling Ivy who carved the candle.

Ella watched on as she made swirls and pretty flowers in her candle. *It's beautiful*, she thought when Ivy showed her the finished candle.

"Now, we are going to light it and when you blow it out, make a wish for your aunt. But believe that it will come true."

Ivy lit the candle, and Ella thought of her wish. *I wish Aunt Rachel will get better soon and that we can play like we did before.* She blew out the candle just as her parents came to fetch her.

"Remember, Ella. The magic is always inside of you. You just need to believe and trust in it," Ivy whispered in her ear as they walked to her mom and dad.

Ella said goodbye to Ivy, held her candle close, and hoped her wish would come true.

***

The next week, Ella and her parents went to visit her Aunt Rachel in the hospital. Her aunt smiled when she walked into her room.

"Aunt Rachel!" Ella shouted happily.

"Ella, darling! I've missed you!" Her aunt hugged her tight and kissed her forehead.

"I've missed you, too," Ella said

"Guess what?"

"What?"

"I'm getting better! Soon I can go home and we can play again."

"Really?" Ella said hopefully.

"Really!"

Ella and Rachel laughed and hugged each other.

"Ella, honey. Be careful with your aunt, okay?" Her mom came into the room and Ella smiled at her.

Ella told her parents about Aunt Rachel getting better and her mom cried. Everyone was glad and couldn't wait for her to come out of the hospital.

Her parents and aunt were talking while Ella looked out the window. She thought about Ivy and her candle

that was sitting in her bedroom. *My wish came true!*

In the window, Ella saw a picture of Ivy come out of it. Her red hair was blowing around like she was standing in the wind. Ivy smiled at her, and she was shocked. Ella looked closer at the window and saw Ivy put a finger to her lip, telling Ella that she needed to be quiet.

Ivy then wiggled her fingers, and the glitter came out of them before she disappeared in a twirl.

Ivy is magic!

Ella wondered at everything that the strange woman had taught her. She looked back at her happy family and now knew that wishes *do* come true!

Once again, Ella believed in magic!

Nurturing Nature

"Grandma!"

"Oh, Emily! There you are!" Emily ran to her grand-mother and gave her a big hug.

The bright sun was shining down on them, and it was one of Emily's favorite days to spend with her grandma in the garden.

Her Grandma Irene loved to look after the small garden she had in the backyard of her home. Every time Emily came over, there were more flowers and plants to look at! The garden was full of color, and Emily was thrilled when she could play in it.

"Did you buy some new flowers?" Emily asked excitedly.

"Yes! And not just flowers, but some vegetables, too," her Grandma replied.

"Cool!" Emily looked around at all the different pots that her Grandma had bought. "Can I help you plant them?"

"I would love it if you could help me. You know, you're my favorite gardening partner." Grandma Irene smiled at her granddaughter and put her gloves back on.

"Thanks, Grandma!" Emily dashed to the cupboard where her grandma kept her gardening stuff and found the pair of pink gloves she used when she was here.

Running back to the spot where they were planting, Emily looked around at some of the flowers she passed. There were bright yellow ones, deep blue ones, bursting pink and purple ones. There were so many, and Emily loved them all!

"Don't forget your cap!" Grandma Irene called, and Emily ran back to the cup-board to get it.

Her mom had tied up her long brown hair this morn-ing, so it was easy for her to put the cap on. Grandma Irene always made sure that she was protected from the sun because it could be *harmful.* She wasn't sure what that

word meant, but she knew that too much sun could be bad for you.

"I got my cap and my gloves!" Grandma Irene smiled at an excited Emily as the little girl put her gloves on.

"Good girl! Okay, so here is what we're going to do. I'm going to tell you which plant to bring over. I'm going to dig the hole and then you're going to help me put it in."

"Okay, Grandma," Emily said and fetched the first plant that she was told to get.

There were bees and birds flying around them as they worked to get all the plants in the right spot. When Emily sat next to her grandma to put the flower in the hole, there was a bee buzzing around her.

"Go away," she mumbled as she concentrated on her task.

But the bee didn't leave her alone. It flew over and under her. Buzzed around and around the spot where they sat. Emily wasn't happy about the bee being there and was scared that she would get stung.

"Leave me alone!" she shouted at the bee when it came too close to her.

"Emily? What's the matter?" Grandma Irene asked and looked at her.

"There's a bee that won't leave me alone. I don't like bees."

"A bee? Why don't you like bees?"

"Because they make irritating sounds and they sting you. It hurts and I don't like it. I wish they were never here." Emily sat down on the ground again and sulked.

Grandma Irene moved from her spot and came closer to Emily. Together, they sat watching the animals in the garden. Emily heard her grandma sigh and looked at her sad face.

"What's wrong, Grandma?"

"Do you know what the word 'extinct' means?"

"Not really."

"It means that there is no longer any type of that animal left in the world," Grandma Irene said.

"Like we will never find them again?" Emily asked.

"Yes, exactly like that. And did you know that bees are very close to becoming that?"

"What do you mean?" Emily faced her grandma and looked into her eyes from under her cap.

"It means that many people are like you and they don't like bees. So they get rid of them instead of saving them."

"Why do we need to save them?" Emily was confused. She looked at the bees that flew above her grandma's head and listened to what she was saying.

"Bees are very important to the environment, Emily. They help all these beautiful plants and flowers grow which also helps the animals. They help us too, because they help the fruits and vegetables grow for us to eat."

"But, Grandma, how do they help?"

"Come with me. I want to show you something." Grandma Irene stood up and walked toward her house.

Emily followed her grandma and stepped into the cool living room. She took off her cap and gloves then went to wash her hands. That was the rule in the house.

"Emily, come into the kitchen."

Emily walked to where her grandma was standing and climbed onto the chair next to her.

Grandma Irene had opened a book on the kitchen counter. The page was filled with different pictures of bees and had some words on it too.

"This book is all about the important animals and insects we need in nature to help it grow. Bees are here as one of the most important insects." Grandma Irene pointed to one picture where a bee was flying around a group of different flowers.

"What's this one?" Emily pointed to one where the bee was sitting on a flower.

"This tells us why they're important. Bees help pollinate the environment. This means that they take the seeds from flowers and spread them around to plant new ones and help other ones grow."

"Wow! That's so cool!"

"It really is. We wouldn't have some of the delicious

fruits and vegetables or the beautiful flowers we have if we didn't have bees." Grandma Irene pointed to a few more pictures on the page.

The bees fascinated Emily. She looked at all the pictures and read the information as best as she could. Her grandma helped as they read through the rest of the book.

Emily learned about birds, beetles, worms, butterflies, and many more! *They do so much*, Emily thought when they finished the last page.

"Nature is huge, Grandma."

"It is. So now you know that everything is useful in nature. Especially bees." Her grandma tapped Emily's nose.

They laughed and had some cold lemonade before Emily and Grandma Irene went back out into the garden.

"Grandma, look! There's one of the birds we saw in the book!" Emily pointed up high into a tree where a small bird sat on a branch.

Grandma Irene squinted her eyes in the afternoon sun to see the bird better. "Would you look at that? Isn't it beautiful?"

"It's really beautiful. I like the color of its feathers," Emily said as she watched the bird fly away.

The bird was small and blue. Its feathers blended together and had a dark blue at the bottom, and as it went up, the blue got lighter.

"Emily, sweetie, would you fetch that red rose over there?" Her grandma pointed to a pot that was filled with beautiful red roses.

"These are beautiful, Grandma. They smell nice too!" she said when she picked up the rose.

Grandma Irene chuckled at Emily as she took the rose and planted it in the ground where they had already dug a hole.

Emily and her grandma spent the rest of the day planting all the flowers and vegetable plants that they had. The sun was setting when they finished and cleaned up before they went back into the house.

Her parents and older sister had come over for dinner and Emily told them about what she learned. Her grandpa, who was playing golf all day, asked her a lot of questions about the book they read.

Emily was really excited when she answered correctly and knew her grandparents were proud of her. Her parents were too.

They were eating the chocolate cake that her mom made for dessert when Emily tapped Grandma Irene on the shoulder.

"Yes, Emily?"

"Thank you for telling me about the bees and the other animals, Grandma."

"You're very welcome. I'm glad you enjoyed learning about them."

Emily nodded her head happily. "I did! I really loved the stuff about the bees. I'm sorry I was so mean to them before."

Emily looked down at her slice of cake, upset. She was sad that she had been so mean to the bee that was flying around her. *I wish there was a way I could talk to them…*

Grandma Irene kindly rubbed Emily's shoulder. "Don't be sad. They know you're sorry and are happy

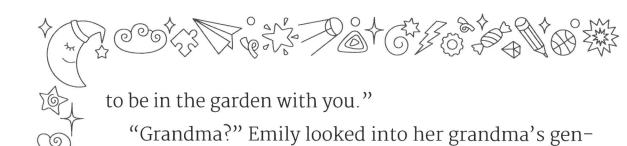

to be in the garden with you."

"Grandma?" Emily looked into her grandma's gentle eyes.

"Yes, Emily?" she said with a smile.

"I think I like bees now."

"I do too."

Emily and Grandma Irene smiled at each other and ate some of the cake.

The rest of their family was laughing and telling jokes. Emily joined and made up a joke about her and the bees in the garden. They were now her forever favorite animal.

Swim With Me!

Layla and her family arrived at the big Ocean Park early one weekend morning. Her two older brothers jumped out of the car first, excited to finally be at their favorite place.

They had been begging their parents to bring them to Ocean Park. Layla was just as excited as her brothers. She quickly jumped out of the car and buzzed with the energy that she had been saving for this day.

"Alright, kids!" her dad called. "Let's grab our gear and go!"

Layla's dad had a huge smile on his face too. When she saw how happy everyone in her family was, she knew it was going to be a fun day.

"Layla, sweetie. Come hold mommy's hand," her mom said.

She walked to her mom and grabbed her hand. Layla thought that she was old enough to walk by herself, but her mom liked to hold hands. Still, she was way too

excited to get into the park and see all the animals and rides!

There were some people around, but not a lot. Her family moved quickly through the line and soon, they walked into the gigantic park. Layla's eyes opened in wonder.

Although they often spoke about coming to this place, it was her first time here. *She was finally old enough and tall enough to go on all the rides.*

Her brothers were talking really fast and over the other, wanting to go on everything all at once. Layla didn't know which one she wanted to do first because she felt a bit scared. But she wouldn't tell anyone that. They would make her stay behind.

"Look around for a nice spot to put our things," her mom said from next to her.

"Over there under those trees. That looks like a good spot." Layla followed her dad and brothers with her mom still holding her hand.

They laid their towels and blankets on the ground, using their bags to make sure that they wouldn't fly away if some wind blew.

"Gather around, everyone. Niel and Marco, calm down. We're here for the whole day, and I'm sure you can go on as many rides as you want." Her mom chuckled at the two boys.

Layla's dad checked their bags to make sure everything was safe, then stood with them.

"So for the rest of the morning, you get to do what you want. Boys, you will need to stick together and come and find us if you need anything or something is wrong. Your dad and I will be with Layla."

"But, Mom, can't I go with them? Please?" she asked nicely. Layla hoped her mom would let her go with her brothers.

"I'm sorry, honey. That was the deal when we said we would come. Maybe next time, but for your first

time, I just want to make sure you're okay and safe."

Layla nodded her head and stuck a tongue out at her brothers who were teasing her.

"Boys, stop," their father warned.

"We'll come back here for lunch and a rest. After that, we get to swim with the dolphins!" her mom said.

Layla, Marco, and Neil all cheered. Swimming with the dolphins was one thing they all wanted to do, and Layla couldn't wait!

When her dad said it was okay, her brothers rushed off to one of the many rides. Layla's mom helped her take off the dress she was wearing over her blue swimming suit. It was the one she liked the most. It had pictures of stars and clouds on it and always made her think of the sky.

Next, her mom quickly braided her red hair to keep it out of her face. After they changed into their swimming suits, they headed for the first ride Layla wanted to try.

Her first time was scary, and it took her a while to go down it. But after that, she was ready to go down all the rides!

Layla had a lot of fun with her parents. They saw her brothers on some rides that they went on and spent the rest of the morning exploring the park.

As her mom said, they came back to their spot for lunch that she had helped her mom make. It was ham and cheese sandwiches with some chips, sliced apples, and juice. The three children talked about their favorite rides and which ones they wanted to go on again after seeing the dolphins.

When they were ready, Layla and her family walked over to the dolphin pool. There were people already swimming with them—some playing and some feeding the dolphins.

"I'm so ready for this!" Marco shouted and Neil cheered with him.

Her brothers ran in first, with her mom following them. Her dad walked with her as she stared at the many dolphins in the pool.

She wanted to play with them, but she was scared to touch them.

"Dad, I'm scared," she said to him.

"You don't have to be scared, sweetie. Dolphins are very friendly and kind. I promise you are going to have

fun!" He gave her a soft pull on her hair braid and went to speak with her mom and someone who worked at the pool.

They were given life jackets and her dad helped to make sure hers was on properly. Then the trainer told them to follow her and Layla's family walked into the pool.

Layla was still scared, so she sat on the edge of the pool and watched her family play with some dolphins.

One silver one swam close to her and popped its head out of the water. It looked at Layla and she didn't move.

"You look scared," she heard it say.

"You can talk?" Layla said, surprised.

"Yes. I can speak to people. I guess it's like a special gift or something."

"So you can understand me?" Layla asked and watched the dolphin swim closer to her.

"Sure can!"

"That's cool. My name's Layla."

"I'm Whiskers. I like your name, Layla. So why are you scared?" Whiskers splashed some water into the air with its tail.

"I don't know. I haven't done anything like this before." Layla looked at her laughing family and wanted to join them.

"Can you swim?"

She looked at the dolphin again and nodded her head yes. "I can swim. I'm just scared to touch you, I think."

"Don't be scared! Come on! I like to play with people. It'll be fun. I promise." Whiskers swam closer to her, a smile on its long snout.

"I don't know..." Layla was still wary.

"Can I tell you a story?" the dolphin asked.

"Okay."

"When I was a little dolphin, I got stuck in some bad things in the ocean. I was really badly hurt and had to come here to get some help. When I was all better, they wanted to bring me back to the ocean, but because of how bad it was, I wouldn't be able to live there on my own. So I stayed here."

"Really?" Layla felt less scared as Whiskers told his story.

"Yep! All of us dolphins here were rescued but can't go back to the sea. So we stay here and have fun with people like you. I was scared too when it was my first time playing with someone else."

"What did you do?" Layla asked.

"One of my trainers helped me by guiding me slowly to the person. When we started playing, I wasn't scared anymore."

Layla looked at her family again and then back at Whiskers. She really wanted to play with him and her family. *She needed to be brave like her parents always told her she was.*

"Here. Hold on to my fin and we will swim out slowly." Whiskers was now right beside her.

Layla took a deep breath, wrapped her hands around the fin, and kicked off from the wall. They slowly swam to the place where the rest of her family was. Everyone smiled at her and she felt a lot better!

Soon, Layla was no longer afraid. She had a lot of fun playing with Whiskers. The dolphin was very kind and funny, splashing her with its tail a lot because she liked it the most.

When their time was over, Layla swam back to the edge of the pool with Whiskers.

"That was so much fun!" she excitedly said.

"I told you! Will you come back soon, Layla?"

"Yes, I will! I promise I'll come play with you again,

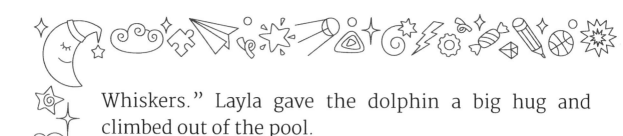

Whiskers." Layla gave the dolphin a big hug and climbed out of the pool.

Her mom held out a towel for her and wrapped her up in it. When they got back to their bags, Marco and Neil ran off for another ride.

Layla was tired after her long day, so she stayed with her mom and dad on the blanket. They were reading and slowly packing up, but Layla was staring at the pool where the dolphins were.

She was exhausted but had a lot of fun that day. Layla even made a new friend—Whiskers the dolphin.

Practice Makes Perfect

Ballet class was Chloé's favorite time of the week. She loved watching all her friends move into different positions. They were all so different from each other, but each time they changed into the called stance, they became one.

"First position!" Ms. Amy called to the class, and all the little ballerinas stood up straight and tall.

"Second position!" she called again, and Chloé spread her arms and legs as instructed.

Ms. Amy continued to call out the different positions for the class to practice. They all stood against the barre and the mirror reflected the girls and their movements.

"That was good, girls. Now I want you to line up in your rows and we're going to work through the sequence we started working on last week."

Chloé and some of her best friends hurried to the front line. They were the top dancers in the 11-12 age

group at Ms. Amy's ballet school. She started ballet when she was three years old and quickly advanced to where she was now.

She smiled at her reflection in the opposite mirror as her teacher began the countdown. As one, the group of 15 girls practiced the routine that was set as part of the upcoming recital they were doing.

They ended the routine with a coupé and a sauté. Chloé's breath came out hard, but she didn't let it show. She looked like the perfect ballerina.

"Nice job, ladies. Remember to keep those toes pointed. We don't want to see slacking feet." Ms. Amy

came around the front of the class as she circled around the group when they were rehearsing.

"Isabella, remember your extensions, okay? You want to be out there, not in here." Ms. Amy showed the opening of her chest with each arm extension to Isabella—Chloé's best friend with her blue eyes and brown hair.

She watched as her teacher and

Isabella practiced and the other girls stood by quietly. This was normal for the class. Each time they finished a piece, their teacher would come around and help those she saw needed extra work.

Chloé wasn't normally one of those people, but there were a few positions that she still struggled to finish properly. The grand jeté was one of them. It was the position where they did a jump into a split in the air.

She tried to stretch and practice her splits every night, but most times, she forgot about it. Ms. Amy said she wouldn't be able to do a grand jeté without being able to do the splits.

"Chloé." Ms. Amy moved over to her. "Have you been practicing?"

Chloé looked down at the floor, embarrassed. "Not really."

"Remember what we talked about? You need that flexibility to be able to extend your body the way it needs to for the different positions. When you extend your leg, I can see it coming here instead of here."

Her teacher stretched her leg out and showed her where Chloé's leg was ending and where it needed to end. It was a lot higher than Chloé could reach right now.

"I want you to practice as often as you can. You're the most advanced student in this class, Chloé, but this could keep you from getting the lead role in the recital like I know you want to." Ms. Amy gave her a kind smile before moving on to the next person.

Chloé walked over to Isabella as she practiced her arm extensions. "I feel so embarrassed."

"Don't be. We all have things we need to work on. I mean, look at me. Who still struggles to extend their *arms*? It's like the most basic thing we're taught." Isabella sighed.

"I know. That's me with my legs. I keep forgetting to practice."

"Me too. I guess we're going to have to practice really hard now if we want the lead in the recital." Chloé nodded her head and shrugged her shoulders when Ms.

Amy called their attention.

"Okay, class is almost over. I want to show you some of the routine that the lead dancer will be doing. Watch carefully for those who are auditioning for it. I'll also hand out a sheet with the steps for you to practice at home."

Chloé, Isabella, and the rest of the girls watched as their teacher moved through the routine beautifully. When it came close to the end, Chloé felt sad as the last steps were a pirouette into a grand jeté.

"Oh no, I'm never going to get the part," she whispered to her friend when Ms. Amy finished.

Chloé picked up her bag that was next to her friend's, and they walked to the door together. Ms. Amy handed out the sheet of paper, but paused when Chloé got to her.

"Can you stay behind for a bit?" she asked.

She stepped to the side of her teacher and waited until everyone had left the studio. Ms. Amy looked at her, and Chloé knew what she was going to say.

"Are you ready to practice properly to get this role?"

"Yes, Ms. Amy."

"Good. I know you can do it. You just have to believe

in yourself. I know this routine is a bit more complicated, but you can nail it. Just keep practicing your splits and grand jeté. You have a month before the audition. It'll be hard, but you can do it."

With a smile and a promise, Chloé left ballet feeling determined to get the lead role. *Just keep practicing...*

***

It had been a week, and Chloé was still struggling to get the move right.

She had done her stretches and practiced every night. She even practiced in the mornings a bit, but she wasn't getting it.

It was a Sunday, and her mom and uncle were inside talking. Chloé stood in the garden, stretching some more to try to do the move.

Something flashed by the corner of their fence and Chloé walked over there to see what it was. It wasn't something but *someone.*

"Hello?" Chloé asked the stranger.

It was a girl that wore a pretty pink leotard and a sparkling white tutu. She had on ballet slippers and her long blond hair held a glowing crown.

"Hello, Chloé." The stranger smiled at her.

"Um, who are you? How do you know my name?"

"I'm Princess Aurora and I saw you were having some trouble with your ballet routine. I thought I could help you as I'm a ballerina too."

"Princess Aurora? Like Sleeping Beauty?" Chloé looked at the pretty lady and wondered if she was real.

The princess laughed. "Oh no. I'm a different princess. I'm a princess of ballerinas. That's why I know your name."

Chloé slowly walked over to Princess Aurora and touched her arm. "You're real!" she said in amazement.

"I promise you're not dreaming, Chloé. I just came to help you. If you'll let me."

"But why?" Chloé moved back to where she was practicing, and Aurora followed her.

"Because you really want it. I can see that you are trying very hard, but you don't believe that you can do it. I'm here to help show you that you can!"

"I don't know why I can't do it. I'm trying my hardest, but I just can't," she said sadly.

"Chloé, it's more than wanting to do something.

You have to believe you can do it. I'm going to help you to believe that."

Chloé nodded her head and gave Princess Aurora a big smile. They spent the rest of the afternoon practicing and by the time the sun set, Chloé could stretch farther than she ever had before!

She thanked Princess Aurora for all the help. The princess promised to come back the next day and the day after that until Chloé could do the move.

***

For the past few weeks, Chloé worked with Aurora, and she was very close to doing the move.

It was the last day before the audition, and Chloé was nervous. She needed to do it now, otherwise she wouldn't be able to do it at the audition.

"Okay, Chloé. Just how we practiced. Remember to see it. To believe it. You can do it." Princess Aurora gave her an encouraging smile.

Chloé counted down in her head and started the routine. She got every move perfect, and it was almost time for her to do the grand jeté.

As she came out of the pirouette, Chloé took a deep

breath and finally believed she could do it. She took a step and leaped high into the air! She landed in the perfect position.

She did it!

"Oh, that was simply beautiful!" Aurora had tears in her eyes as she clapped for a beaming Chloé.

"I did it, Aurora. I really did it!"

"You did! And it was magnificent! Now do that at your audition tomorrow and you *will* get the lead role." The princess smiled even more.

"Thank you so much! I couldn't have done it without you!" Chloé gave Aurora a hug as she spoke.

"I believe you would've done it without my help, but I'm glad I did. I'm going to have to go now Chloé, but I'll be watching you. Remember to see it and believe it. Good luck tomorrow!"

Before Chloé could say anything, Princess Aurora disappeared into a cloud of sparkling dust.

Chloé was so happy that she landed the move. She ran to her mom and excitedly told her all about it.

At the audition the following day, Chloé remembered everything that Aurora had taught her. She really couldn't have done it without her, so this audition was for her too.

Chloé gave Ms. Amy a determined smile, took a deep breath, and stepped into the first position of the routine.

It wasn't long after that audition that Chloé leaped through the air as the lead dancer, center stage, at their ballet recital. *Hard work really pays off*, she thought when she landed a perfect grand jeté.

Ahoy, Mateys!

Grace searched her closet for all the pirate clothes and toys that she could find. After finishing her homework, Grace saw that her brother and his friend were playing a pirate game and wanted to join them.

She found a pink bandana that she tried to tie around her black hair. In one of the bottom drawers, she found an eye patch and a wooden sword. The last thing she found was a toy bird that she tied to her shoulder as her "pirate matey."

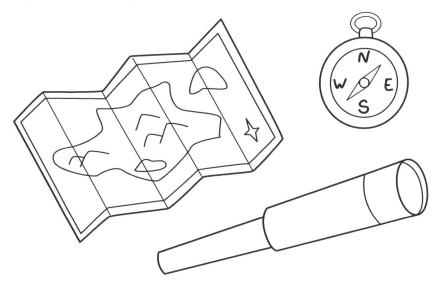

Running out of the house to the play set where the boys were playing, she saw her twin brother Noah walking on a beam. Liam, his best friend, used a spyglass to look for pretend creatures and other pirates.

"Aargh! We have something strange in the water, captain," Liam said as he looked at Grace through the spyglass.

Noah carefully crossed the beam to the other side of the play set, turned, and saw her too. "It's a rascal, me matey. Let's get her!"

"Aye, aye, captain!"

The two boys jumped down from their spot and started chasing her. Grace ran away from them and around the pool. She pulled out her sword from her pants where she put it and raised it at Noah and Liam.

"Don't come any closer or I'll cut you."

"You can't get us. You're a girl!" her brother said in his pirate voice.

"I'll still get you."

"No, you won't." Noah wasn't using his pirate voice anymore. He didn't really want to play with his sister.

"Yes, I will," Grace argued back.

"No, you won't."

"Yes, I will."

Noah and Grace argued for a while before Liam kicked a ball and hit the fence around their yard.

"Noah, can we go back to playing now?"

"Yeah, let's go." They turned back to where they were playing and left Grace behind.

"Wait!" she shouted after them. "I want to play too."

"You can't play with us, Grace," Noah said over his shoulder.

"Why not?"

"Because."

"Because why?" Grace ran after them.

"*Because* I said so!" Her brother tried to ignore her.

"Mom said that you aren't allowed to say that anymore."

"Ugh, fine, whatever." Liam and Noah looked at each other and laughed.

"What's so funny?" Grace asked, confused.

"Nothing, just a joke between us *boys*," Liam said as

he laughed some more.

"Oh, okay. So can I play with you?" she asked again hopefully.

"Hah! No, you can't," her brother said and pushed her out of his way.

Grace watched as the boys climbed back onto the play set. "Please, Noah. I really want to play."

"You're a girl," he scoffed.

"So?" Grace was confused. *Girls can be pirates, too.*

"So... *girls can't play boys' games.*" Liam and Noah laughed loudly again.

They ignored her again and continued playing their game. Grace stood there watching them, sad and hurt by what Noah had said.

He could be mean to her sometimes which always made her upset. They didn't even look at her while they played and when she tried to speak, they talked over her.

Grace stomped her foot and walked away from them. She sulked as she walked into her bedroom and threw her pirate stuff off. The sword hit the wall which her parents wouldn't be happy about, but she didn't care.

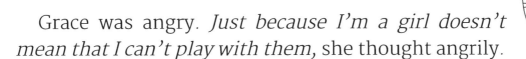

Grace was angry. *Just because I'm a girl doesn't mean that I can't play with them,* she thought angrily.

She wanted to tell her mom about Noah, so she rushed to her parents' office. Grace and Noah's mom worked from home, so it was easy to find her behind her desk.

"Mom?" Grace knocked on the open door to get her mom's attention.

"Yes, hon?" Her mom swirled around in her chair and greeted her with a small smile.

"Noah and Liam won't let me play with them." She crossed her arms and stepped closer to her mother.

"Maybe they just want to have some boy time."

"But Noah said I can't play with them because I'm a girl!" Grace whined and her mother sighed.

"Oh dear. That really wasn't nice of him"

"And then they laughed and ignored me."

"Come here." Grace's mom called her over to her. She did and her mom rubbed her arms in comfort.

"He was being so mean, Mom."

"I know, but listen to me. Girls can do anything boys can do. Just like boys can do anything that girls can.

We're all equal, okay? Don't listen to your brother. He just likes to tease you which we told him not to do because it isn't right."

"What should I do? They still won't let me play with them."

"Well, maybe you could find something else to do? Something better." Her mom smiled at her.

"Like what?" Grace asked.

"Let's think." Her mom lifted her onto her lap and swirled them in her chair.

"Mom, do you think I should do something that they would want to do?"

"I suppose you could. Remember though, Grace, don't do something to spite them. It would be a waste of time. Do something that *you* really enjoy doing. And then if they ask to play with you, ask them to say sorry and then, if you want, you can let them play with you." Her mom said as they swirled some more.

"Okay. I understand. Do you think I can play on the PlayStation for a bit? Noah and Liam always get to play and I never do."

"Maybe after swim practice. Mrs. Turner is going to come pick you up in an hour to take you. I want you to go play outside or something else for now."

"But, Mom!" Grace whined.

"It's nearly time to leave. I promise you can play when you get back. Liam will still be here as his parents are going to be late today. Go on and make sure to be ready before Mrs. Turner gets here," her mom said, speaking about her best friend's mother.

"Yes, Mom." Grace jumped off of her lap.

"Grace? I'm going to speak with your brother and Liam, okay? What they did wasn't right," her mom said.

She nodded at her mom and left the room. Grace stopped at the kitchen sliding door and looked at the boys playing and having fun. Grace felt better after speaking to her mom, but she was still upset. She watched them for a bit and then went to her room.

Grace found a coloring book and sat at her desk until she had to get ready for swim practice. Her mom came

in a while later to tell her that Mrs. Turner would be there soon.

Leaving her crayons and coloring book on her desk, she changed into her swimsuit and her mom tied her hair up into a bun and helped put her swim cap on. When her best friend's mom came, she ran out the door and jumped into the car.

For the next hour, Grace forgot about Noah and Liam. She had a lot of fun with her friends at swim practice and her coaches made her laugh with their funny jokes.

When she got home, her mom told her to take a shower before she played PlayStation. Liam and Noah were still playing outside, but they weren't playing pirates. They were kicking the ball at each other.

Grace showered and changed into her pajamas. She rushed to the living room, switched on the TV and the PlayStation, and made herself comfortable on the sofa.

She chose a racing game that she liked to play and got lost in the world of race cars and crashes.

"Who said you could play?"

Grace jumped and crashed her car in the game.

Noah and Liam had come inside, but she didn't hear

them as she was focused on the screen. They stood behind the sofa and watched her.

"Mom," she said and restarted the game.

"Oh, can we play?" her brother asked.

"I don't know. Are you sure you want to play with a *girl*?" Grace teased.

"Oh. Mom spoke to me when you were at swim practice. She told me it was wrong to say that."

"Okay?"

"I guess I'm saying sorry."

She paused the game and turned to look at her twin brother. He looked embarrassed, and Liam moved awkwardly next to him.

"I'm sorry too," Liam said.

"Did Mom tell you about the boy and girl thing?" she asked them.

"Yeah," Noah said. "I know girls and boys can do the same things. I just didn't want to play

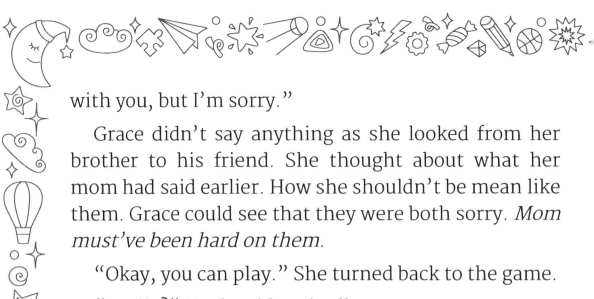

with you, but I'm sorry."

Grace didn't say anything as she looked from her brother to his friend. She thought about what her mom had said earlier. How she shouldn't be mean like them. Grace could see that they were both sorry. *Mom must've been hard on them.*

"Okay, you can play." She turned back to the game.

"Really?" Noah said excitedly.

"Yes, really. Now grab your controls before I start the game again. Otherwise, you're not playing."

Noah and Liam quickly grabbed the spare controls and sat on either side of her. They played the racing game. Grace won most of the races before Liam left.

The next day, Liam came over again to play with Noah and Grace's friend joined them. The boys played the pirate game again and the two girls asked to join.

"Climb aboard, me mateys!" Noah said.

"Aye, aye, captain!" Liam, Grace, and her friend shouted as they fought off pretend rascals on the play set.

Moving On

Riley sat on the outside steps of her old house. She didn't want to move. Her parents were packing the last few boxes into the moving truck. She was supposed to be helping her younger brother and sister to pack their car.

"Come on, Riley. We need to go."

"No, Dad. I don't want to go!" Riley shouted across the driveway.

"We're not doing this again. We're moving and that's final," her dad said, irritated at her whining.

"But I don't want to leave! You do! Why can't we just stay here?" Riley cried and hugged her knees to her chest.

Transferred is what they told her a few months ago. Something to do with his work that Riley didn't really understand. What she knew was that they would have to move. *To another state!*

Riley was 10 years old and was supposed to start middle school in the next few weeks. She had been so excited to go to a new school with all of her friends. They had made promises to stay friends forever and to always be there for each other. But now she would have to start a new school with new friends. *If she made new friends...*

Her mom walked past her, carrying another box. "Riles, be a big girl and come help us. Please?"

"Fine!" she yelled. Riley stood up and wiped the tears on her cheeks.

She stomped inside the empty house and grabbed her bag. Riley walked to the car and angrily opened the door. She dumped her bag on the floor, climbed in, and slammed the door shut.

They had opened the window to let in some air, and she heard her mother sigh at her. She didn't want to move so that she didn't have to help them pack.

"Riley, please." Her mom came to the window. "We know it's hard. It's hard for all of us to leave here, but we have to. It would be easier for the whole family if we *all* helped and tried to be better about the move."

"I don't want to go." Her tears ran down her cheeks.

"I know, baby. I do. And I'm so sorry that we have to, but Daddy's work really needs him to help the company. Your dad and I really need you to be brave and help Emilia and Jack."

As her mom said their names, her younger sister and brother came out the front door with their bags. They looked sad too, but Riley didn't know what they could be sad about. They didn't have to leave all their friends and school behind like she did.

"Riley?" her mom called her again.

She didn't want to be brave for her siblings. She just wanted to stay here.

"Riley?" Again, her mom called, but she would not

talk to her.

Riley's mom took a deep breath and left her alone. Riley didn't move as the rest of their boxes were packed. She didn't speak to her family when they finished packing the car and got in.

When her dad started the car and started to leave, Riley looked back at her old house and wished she could make everything stop.

But she couldn't. No one would listen to her, no matter what she said. So she didn't say anything anymore.

Riley sulked and ignored her family for the entire nine-hour car ride. Emilia and Jack tried to get her to play some car games with her, but she didn't want to. Her mom and dad tried to talk to her nicely, but she still said nothing.

Eventually, they got really upset with her and told Riley that they didn't like the way she was acting. Riley still didn't speak.

It was nighttime when they arrived at their new house. Her dad pulled the car into their new garage and the moving trucks parked in their new driveway.

Riley watched silently from the car as everybody got out and unpacked some boxes. Her mom took her brother and sister inside to set up the cots they were going to sleep in. It was past their bedtime which made Emila and Jack very grumpy.

She was tired too but refused to leave the car. *Maybe if she didn't get out, then it would all be a dream.*

Some time later, Riley fell asleep in the car. She felt someone pick her up and from their smell, she knew it was her dad. As much as Riley wanted to fight him, she was too tired to.

The last thing she remembered from that night was her dad softly laying her on her cot, taking off her shoes, tucking her in, and his whispered word: "I'm so sorry, baby. I love you."

***

The next few days were spent the same way—her parents made her move boxes and unpack. Although she

was too small to move the big ones, they gave her some of the smaller ones for her and her siblings' rooms.

One good thing from this move, Riley thought as she looked through another box in her room. *We all get our own rooms.*

In their old house, Riley and Emila had to share a room while Jack had his own one. But just because she had her own room didn't mean she liked this house more than the other.

But she was *excited* about it.

That afternoon, Riley was tired and didn't want to unpack anymore. Her mom said she could go play outside.

Riley sat on the front step outside and watched as some of her new neighbors walked by. They waved at her and she waved back. Her parents always said to be polite, even if she was sad.

There was nothing she could do and no one to play with. If they were at her old house, Riley could play with her best friends that lived down the next street.

Just then, a girl with brown hair and a boy with red hair came running up to her.

"Hi! I'm Abigail and this is Ben!" the girl said excitedly.

"Hello," the boy, Ben, said with a wave.

"Oh, I'm Riley."

"Cool! I like your name." Abigail smiled brightly at her.

Riley felt weird sitting on the step while they looked down at her. She stood up and stuffed her hands into her packets. She didn't know what to say.

"So you're new here?" Ben asked and looked behind her at all the empty boxes on their front porch.

"I guess," Riley mumbled.

"I think that's awesome!"

Ben nodded his head at what Abigail had said.

"Why? I think it sucks." Riley kicked the ground with her shoe.

"Well, it means you get to make extra friends, doesn't it?" said Ben.

"I had to leave my friends behind. I don't think they're my friends anymore."

"When I moved here, I thought so too. But I talk to

my old friends over the phone all the time. I actually went to visit them last week," said Abigail.

Riley looked at Abigail, shocked.

"You did?"

"Yeah!" The brown-haired girl nodded her head quickly.

Maybe if she asked her parents nicely, they would let her visit her old friends too!

"Do you want to come play with us? I live next door and have a trampoline," Ben asked her.

Riley didn't know what to do. She wanted to play but didn't want to play with anyone but her other friends.

But her mom said she could make new ones.

"I don't know. I'll have to ask my mom and dad." Riley ran inside and called for her parents.

"Mom! Dad!"

"In here, baby!" Riley followed her mom's voice to Emilia's room where they were setting up her bed and everything.

"Can I go next door to play with some friends?"

"Friends? Did you meet some other kids?" her dad asked from where he sat on the floor.

"Sorta. They said their names are Abigail and Ben and that Ben lives next door. He has a trampoline."

"That's great! Let me come with you to meet his parents and if everything's okay, you can go play, okay?" Riley's mom went to wash her hands and then they walked back outside together.

Her mom greeted Abigail and Ben before the group walked over to Ben's house. His family was kind and invited everyone inside. Ben had a younger brother too and the children all went outside to the trampoline while Riley's mom spoke with Ben's parents.

Soon, her mom had to go back next door but said that

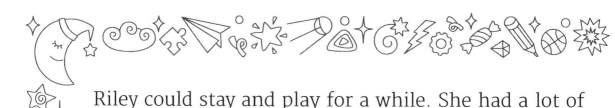

Riley could stay and play for a while. She had a lot of fun playing with Abigail, Ben, and his younger brother.

A while later, Emilia and Jack also came to play. Riley ran back into Ben's house from his backyard and saw both her parents talking with Ben's and who looked like Abigail's mom and dad.

She hurried to her dad and gave him a big hug. He laughed, picked her up, and hugged her tighter.

"What's up?"

"Nothing, dad. I just wanted to say sorry. I know I wasn't happy about the move, but maybe it won't be so bad."

"We know it's hard on you, but I'm sure you will be happy here too." Her mom came over to them and brushed her hair behind her ear.

"Do you think we could go visit my old friends?" Riley asked.

"I'm sure we can do that." Her dad smiled at her.

"Thank you! Love you!" Riley tried to wiggle out of his arms.

"We love you too!" Her parents laughed behind her as she ran back outside and to her new friends.

Sent With Love

"James! Catch!" Stella watched as her oldest twin brothers, James and Lucas, played catch with each other.

They laughed and tried to get the other to catch really hard throws which made her laugh. She turned and looked at her older sister, Aria, as she swung high into the sky on the swing set. Her other older brother, Thomas, was sliding down the slide.

Her family was playing in the park after having a picnic for lunch. Her Aunt Delilah joined them because she didn't have to work that day.

Stella, who was eight years old, couldn't be happier with the family that

she was blessed with. Her parents adopted her when she was four years old after she was left at the fire station where her dad worked.

She didn't see them as her adoptive family because they all made her feel loved like she *was* one of them. Her brothers even teased her like they did with Aria.

"What's up, Stells-bells?" Her Aunt Delilah sat down next to her on the grass.

"Nothing. Just watching."

"Just watching, hey? Well, can I sit and watch with you?"

Stella smiled at her aunt. "Duh!"

Aunt Delilah laughed and nudged Stella's shoulder. They watched as a dog ran past them, chasing a ball that its owner threw far for it to fetch. Stella sat silently and watched all the people move around the park.

"So, are you excited about Valentine's Day?" her aunt asked.

Stella turned and looked at her, and a smile grew on her face. "Yes! It's my favorite holiday!"

"I know! Do you think you're going to get any surprises this year?" Aunt Delilah asked, and the dog ran

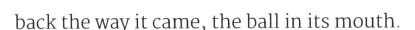

back the way it came, the ball in its mouth.

"I don't know, but I think I want to do something nice for my brothers and sister."

"That's a great idea, Stells!"

"Thank you!" Stella beamed up at her aunt. "I kinda wanted to show them how much they all mean to me, you know? Like after the adoption and all that."

"You know you don't have to do that, Stella. They all love you. *We* love you." Aunt Delilah pulled her into a hug, and Stella hugged her tighter.

"I know. I just want to do something. Also, I think it would be fun!"

"I'd love to help you if you need it," Stella's aunt offered.

"Thank you!" Stella gave her aunt one more hug before she went to play with Thomas and Aria on the play set.

They were laughing and chasing each other a while later when Stella looked over at the pond. The park they were in was big and had a huge pond in the middle of it where ducks liked to swim. Stella loved to feed the ducks when her mom said she could.

"Aria? Do you see something over there?" she asked her older sister.

"Where?"

"By the pond."

"I don't see anything," Aria said, and she went back to playing with Thomas.

Stelle could still see something that hadn't been there before. She slowly walked toward the pond and, as she got closer, she was surprised to see what it was.

It's a unicorn?

Stella was amazed! She didn't know what it was doing here or why nobody else was looking at it. She looked around and, like Aria, no one saw the great big unicorn standing by the water.

"Hello," Stella whispered as she stepped even closer to it.

"You can see me?" the unicorn spoke, surprising Stella.

"Yeah, I can." Stella looked at the magnificent animal.

The unicorn was white with a colorful horn on its head. The horn had different shades of pink, purple,

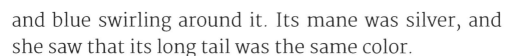

and blue swirling around it. Its mane was silver, and she saw that its long tail was the same color.

"No one has ever seen me before," it said.

"How come I can then?" Stella questioned as she sat on the bench that was near the unicorn.

"I don't know. My name's Sylvie." She couldn't tell if the unicorn was a boy or a girl, but its voice was soft.

"Sylvie? Like your silver hair?"

"Yes!" the unicorn said happily.

"You're so pretty. My name's Stella."

"Thank you, Stella. You look pretty too!" Stella smiled.

"What are you doing here?" she asked.

"Oh! Every year around Valentine's Day, I like to come here to watch the people and the children. I enjoy being around people this time of year," Sylvie sighed wistfully.

"I know what you mean.

Valentine's Day is my favorite holiday."

"It is? Why? A lot of children like Christmas." Sylvie walked closer to Stella.

"I like Christmas too. But Valentine's Day is close to the day I got adopted, so it's always been special to me."

"That's a lovely story, Stella. Are you going to do anything special for it?"

"I was thinking of doing something for my brothers and sister, but I don't know what yet," she said.

Stella reached out a hand and gently patted Sylvie. The unicorn's hair was really soft, and it sparkled where Stella touched it.

"You know, when I was a young unicorn long ago, I heard that people used to write and send each other letters. They always looked so happy when they got a special letter."

"A letter? Don't they come in the mail, though?" Stella thought about all the mail her parents got. *Most of the time they were just bills*, her parents would tell her.

"Maybe you could put it in a mailbox or something.

I'm sure it would make them feel special." Sylvie nudged Stella's hand onto its head to rub there.

Stella thought about Sylvie's idea more and more. *I love it!* she thought as she continued to rub the pretty unicorn.

"Thank you for the idea, Sylvie! I'm going to do it!" Stella jumped off the bench in her excitement.

"I hope they like it. It was nice meeting you, Stella!"

"You're leaving?" the little girl said sadly.

"It's time for me to go, but I see someone calling for you."

Stella looked over her shoulder and saw Aunt Delilah waving at her. She looked back at Sylvie and gave the unicorn a pat goodbye.

"Will I see you again, Sylvie?" Stella asked.

"Yes, you will!"

"Okay! Goodbye, Sylvie!" Stella waved as the unicorn walked away.

"Stella!"

She turned to see her aunt getting closer and when she looked back to where the unicorn had been, she saw that it had disappeared.

"Stella! What are you doing all the way here?" Aunt Delilah asked when she reached her niece.

"I was just looking at the ducks and thinking about my Valentine's Day gift."

"Did you have an idea?" Stella and her aunt walked back to her family.

"Yeah, I did! I'm going to write them letters and send them in the mail. Like they used to do in the old days."

"Hey! It wasn't that long ago," Aunt Delilah chuckled and playfully messed up Stella's hair. "I love it, although Valentine's is in two days and I don't think the mail will get here in time."

"Oh," Stella whispered. "What do you think we should do?"

"Well, I saw these tiny mailboxes at the store the other day. Maybe we could get one for everyone and you can put your letter in there."

"Yes! And maybe we could get some candy or chocolate as an extra treat!" Stella jumped with excitement.

"Now you're talking, Stells!" Aunt Delilah smiled. "But what about you? Don't you want anything special?"

"Nah! I just want my family to feel special."

***

The following day, Aunt Delilah picked Stella up to go shopping for the tiny mailboxes. Her aunt told her parents that she was babysitting for the day while her brothers and sister were visiting with friends.

They giggled when they got into her aunt's car and talked about their Valentine's surprise the whole way over to the store.

Aunt Delilah showed her the way to the mini mailboxes, and Stella looked at them in awe. There were so many colors!

She got a different color for each person in her family. Red for her dad, white for her mom, green and blue for James and Lucas, pink for Aria, orange for Thomas, and a purple one for Aunt Delilah.

Next, they walked down the candy aisle looking for the perfect treat to go into the mailboxes. Aunt Delilah found some heart-shaped chocolates and Stella found some candy that said "I love you." They got both!

Stella was so excited about the surprise that she didn't see Aunt Delilah put in an extra little silver mailbox.

They drove to her aunt's house where Stella spent the afternoon writing the letters to each person in her family. She was still learning to spell and write, so Aunt Delilah helped her with the letters.

When the letters were finished, they packed the mailboxes and drove back to Stella's house where they had dinner with her family. Aunt Delilah promised to stay after the children went to bed to put out the mailboxes as a surprise for them when they woke up in the morning.

And it was a surprise! Everyone was so happy to see the mailboxes on the morning of Valentine's Day.

Stella gave each one their colors, leaving the purple one for her aunt when she came over later. They all opened the mailboxes and read the letters when Stella saw the silver one.

It looked like Sylvie's hair. She quickly opened it and

found a letter from her aunt telling her how much she loved her. Stella found the candy and something else in the mailbox—unicorn stickers!

Did Aunt Delilah know about Sylvie?

Stella forgot her thought when her whole family wrapped her up in one big hug.

"We love you, Stella!" her parents and siblings said together.

Stella laughed in happiness. This is what she wanted. They were all happy!

Snowflake's Story

Skylar stared at the board as Mrs. Wilson wrote down the date for the deadline of the story competition.

It was coming up soon and if she wanted to enter a story, Skylar would have to start it that very day. Except she couldn't bring herself to write anything.

There was a part of her that didn't know what to write about. And another part that didn't think she was good enough to enter the contest.

Skylar sighed and rested her chin on her hand. Mrs. Wilson, her teacher, turned back to the class with a warm smile.

"As you can see, the deadline is coming up pretty fast, so those of you who want to enter but still haven't, you need to do so now." Her teacher looked right at Skylar and she sat up straight.

She knew Mrs. Wilson wanted her to enter a story, and she didn't want to disappoint her. For the rest of class, Skylar thought about the story contest instead of paying attention to the lesson.

It was the last lesson of the day, so when the bell rang, all the students hurriedly packed up their bags and ran out the door when Mrs. Wilson dismissed them. But she stopped Skylar when she tried to sneak out.

"Skylar? Can we talk for a minute?" Mrs. Wilson kindly smiled at her.

She knew what her teacher wanted to talk about and felt ashamed that she couldn't say yes to the competition yet. For all the thinking she did in class about it, she didn't know what to write about.

"Yes, Mrs. Wilson?"

"How's your story coming along? I haven't seen it entered yet."

Skylar moved her backpack from one shoulder to the other. "I haven't written it exactly…"

"Oh," her teacher said in surprise. "Are you not wanting to enter a story?"

"No, I do." Skylar looked at Mrs. Wilson as her teacher stared back at her, but she didn't say anything.

"Okay... Is something wrong? Are you having trouble with anything?" Mrs. Wilson gestured for Skylar to have a seat at a nearby desk.

Skylar sat down and Mrs. Wilson sat at the desk next to her.

"It's just that I don't really know what to write about and if I'm even good enough for the competition," Skylar whispered sadly.

"Skylar, you are a very talented story writer. One of the best in your grade, in fact. I guarantee you will do very well in the contest."

"But, Mrs. Wilson, what would I even write about? I've tried to think of something, but nothing seems good enough!" she whined.

"Alright, well, let us both think for a minute. A good story is one that comes from the heart, right?"

Skylar nodded her head. "You also said during class something about it being meaningful?"

"That's correct. A good story comes from the heart and is meaningful to you. Bringing out that deeper meaning in it will help others see the story like you do. So you should find something to write about that means a lot to you."

Mrs. Wilson gave her another kind smile while Skylar thought about different story ideas.

"So like my friends and family?" she asked her.

"Yes, that's one idea. Though between you and me, a lot of people wrote about that, so if you want to stick out, find something that really is personal to *you.*"

"Personal to me?" Skylar repeated to herself. *What is personal to me?*

They sat in silence for a moment while Skylar tried to come up with her idea. Her face lit up when something came to her!

"My cat, Snowflake!" she said excitedly.

"Snowflake?" her teacher asked.

"Yes! He was this black and white cat I had when I was younger. He was my best friend, but passed away last year. He meant a lot to me and I was really sad when he died."

"I think that's perfect, Skylar."

"Thanks, Mrs. Wilson!" Skylar jumped up from her

seat, excited to write about her cat. "See you tomorrow!"

"Bye, Skylar!" her teacher called behind her.

Skylar ran to the gate where her babysitter was waiting for her. During the car ride home, she told her babysitter all about her idea for her story and how she was going to work on it all afternoon.

And she did! Well, mostly…

She had to take a break to go to her Girl Scouts meeting, but as soon as she was back, Skylar was back to writing.

It wasn't supposed to be a long story, but it took her a while to write it. Skylar would start and then throw that piece of paper away before trying again on a new page. She just couldn't get the right words.

It took some time and some encouragement from her babysitter, but she finally found the words she liked. By the time her parents came home, she was halfway finished with the story.

They made her stop for the night though because she hadn't done all her other homework. After she finished her homework, had dinner, and then had a bath, Skylar tried to sneak her story into her bed, but her mom caught her.

"I promise you can finish it tomorrow, but it's bedtime now," her mom said and took the paper out of her hand.

Her parents wished her sweet dreams before turning off the bedroom light. Skylar closed her eyes and pictures of Snowflake were in her dreams. When she woke the next morning, he was all she could think about.

Skylar's school day went by slowly. All she wanted to do was go home and finish her story.

Her wish came true when the last bell rang and she rushed out of the classroom with everyone else. As soon as she got home, Skylar went straight to her desk and wrote down all the things she thought of during the day.

Luckily, she didn't have any activities to go to that afternoon, and her babysitter helped her when she needed it. Skylar had just finished the last sentence

when her parents got home and her babysitter left.

"How's the story going?" her mom asked as she gave her a hug.

"Good! I just finished it!" Skylar smiled with pride.

"Can we hear some of it?" her father asked this time.

"Okay!" Skylar quickly got the paper she wrote on and stood in front of her parents who sat on the sofa.

She took a deep breath in and began to read.

"I remember when we first met. I was just a baby and I'm still a child, but I knew it was love at first sight. You licked my face with your tickling pink tongue and I giggled. Your spotted fur looked like the night sky.

From that point on, you weren't just a cat. You were my cat. You were my Snowflake.

We had a lot of fun times, you and I. Running through the yard and climbing up giant trees. I used to get into so much trouble from Mom and Dad when I followed you up there.

I haven't climbed a tree since you left and I haven't gotten into trouble either. Maybe that's a good thing as I haven't been as grounded as much as I used to be. But I miss you.

I miss you more than the sun misses the moon. More than Dad misses Mom when she has a work trip. More than I miss chocolate when I can't have it.

You were my Snowflake. You will always be my Snowflake."

Skylar finished reading the rest of the story for her parents before she sheepishly looked up at them. Her mom had tears in her eyes and her dad had a proud smile on his face.

"I think that's the best story you've ever written, Sky." Her dad clapped his hands and her mom joined.

"Your dad's right. That was beautiful!"

"Mrs. Wilson said to write from the heart and I love Snowflake so..."

"It's perfect! And I'm sure Mrs. Wilson will love it too." Her mom called her over to sit between them.

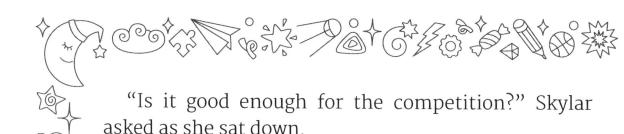

"Is it good enough for the competition?" Skylar asked as she sat down.

"It's more than good enough. I promise." Her mom gave her a reassuring smile.

"But what if I don't win?"

"Skylar, it's not about winning," her dad started. "It's about bringing your story to life so that other people can have a chance to experience it. You may not win, but you know you did your best and wrote from the heart. No one can take that away from you."

Her dad's words stuck with her the next day as she walked into Mrs. Wilson's class.

"Here you go Mrs. Wilson. I finished my story." Skylar handed the piece of paper to her teacher.

"That's wonderful! Thank you." Her teacher smiled at her, and Skylar walked to her desk.

She saw Mrs. Wilson read over her story and smiled when her teacher looked at her. "Skylar, this is amazing. I'm so proud of you."

"Thank you. I wrote from the heart like you taught me to."

"You sure did. Well done!"

Skylar couldn't stop smiling. Even if she didn't win, Snowflake would always be number one in her heart.

My Fairy Godmother

"But, Grandma! Can't we make it better or something?" Caroline whined as she looked in the mirror.

It was Halloween tomorrow and because it was going to be a Saturday, her school said they could wear their costumes on Friday.

"I'm sorry, buttercup, but this is all I could do." Her grandma straightened the coat she was wearing, but Caroline was still upset.

She wanted to go as a firefighter and looked forward to having all the cool stuff that firefighters had. What she was wearing was not what she wanted.

Her grandma promised she would do the best that she could, but they didn't have a lot of money. Caroline's costume was homemade.

"Everyone else is going to have a new costume but me." She stomped her feet which were in a pair of her old boots. They were not like the ones firefighters wore.

"Caroline." Her grandma grabbed her shoulders

and turned her to look into her eyes. "I know this isn't what you wanted, but remember that grandma said she would try her best."

"I know. I just wanted something cool like the other kids." There were tears in Caroline's brown eyes and her grandma gently wiped them away.

"Do you know what I think makes you cool?" her grandma said quietly.

Caroline shook her head no.

"You don't need all those new clothes and costumes. You're cool enough all on your own."

She didn't want to smile, but when her grandma tickled her sides, Caroline laughed and gave her a hug.

"Thank you, grandma."

"That's a good girl. Now, grab your backpack and off to school you go." Caroline gave her a quick hug before she got her bag and left for school.

She was lucky that her grandma's house was down the road from her school. When Caroline came to live with her, her grandma still walked her to school. Now that she was 10 years old, she could walk by herself.

Caroline liked the look of the trees. It was fall and all the leaves were turning orange and red. Those were her favorite colors. There was one tree she liked the most.

It had big, wide branches that Caroline always thought would be the best to climb. It was also the tree that still had most of its leaves while the others had been falling off.

That morning though, there was something else in the tree. She didn't know what it was, but it was big. *Huge.*

Maybe someone built a treehouse in it? she thought as she got closer.

But it wasn't a treehouse. When Caroline stood right by the tree, the big thing looked like a carriage!

She thought it was weird for that to be in a *tree*, but she shrugged her shoulders and took a step along her path.

Caroline was still a bit sad about her costume, though there wasn't anything she could do about it.

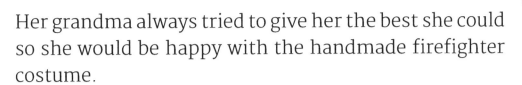

Her grandma always tried to give her the best she could so she would be happy with the handmade firefighter costume.

Just then, she heard a noise from up in the tree. Caroline thought it could be a bird, so she looked up to see if she could find it. What she found wasn't a bird.

"Woo-hoo! Caroline!" the person in the tree sang.

Caroline looked around, but there wasn't anyone else on the street. She looked back up at the person.

"Are you talking to me?" she asked.

"Yes! I've been waiting all morning for you!" The person floated down from the branch and landed right in front of her.

Caroline saw that it wasn't just any person. It was a lady that sort of looked like her grandma!

"I'm not supposed to talk to strangers," Caroline said as she took a step back.

"I agree with you. You're not supposed to talk to

strangers, but I'm not a stranger! I'm your fairy god-mother—Eve!" The lady smiled brightly at her.

Caroline looked at the fairy dress she was wear-ing and how there were sparkles in the air every time she moved. She also saw a sparkly wand in one of her hands. *Maybe she really is a fairy godmother...*

"If you're my fairy godmother, how come I haven't seen you before?" she asked, curious.

"Well, I only come to you when you really need me. Like today!"

"What's so special about today?"

"A little birdie told me you wanted a new firefighter costume for Halloween," Eve said.

"I did." Caroline looked down at the ground. "But it's okay if I have this one. My grandma tried, I guess."

"She tried her best, I promise you. That's why I'm here! I'm going to give you your true firefighters cos-tume!" Eve the fairy godmother spread her arms and twirled in a circle.

"Really?" Caroline said excitedly.

"Yes! Are you ready?"

Caroline nodded her head quickly and smiled as

Eve waved her magic wand in the air. Everywhere she looked, she saw the sparkles moving.

When they disappeared, Caroline looked at her costume and squealed. "It's the best firefighter costume ever!"

It really was! The coat and pants were the same color as the ones she saw on real firefighters. She had the helmet, boots, and toy hose to go along with it!

"Oh my gosh! Thank you! Thank you! I love it!" Caroline rushed to hug Eve who chuckled as she hugged her back.

"You are most certainly welcome!"

"Eve, what did I do that made you come here?" She pulled back from the hug and looked up at her fairy godmother.

Eve smiled down at her. "When your grandma said she couldn't do anything else, you were sad, but you also appreciated that she tried."

"What does *appreciated* mean?" Caroline sat down on the side of the sidewalk.

Her fairy godmother sat down next to her and smoothed out her dress. "It means that you knew she would do anything for you and give you her best. You were sad, but you were okay with it."

"Oh. But Eve, what can I do for you to say thank you? My grandma says I should always see what I can do for others."

"She sounds like a good grandma." Eve picked up an orange leaf that fell off the tree and played with it.

"She's the best!" Caroline said with the biggest smile on her face.

"I'm happy about that! There isn't really anything you can do for me, but I want you to remember something."

"Okay." Caroline fixed her bag that was on her back. She had to move it with the new costume she was wearing.

"I want you to always remember to be kind to others. Having wonderful things yourself is great, but helping others is even better."

Caroline nodded her head. Her grandma taught her the same thing, but she made a promise to Eve to always do that too.

"I promise, Eve."

"Good! You better hurry along, Caroline, or you might be late for school."

They both stood up from the sidewalk and Caroline gave Eve another hug. "When can I see you again?"

"Oh, you'll see me soon enough. Run along, sweet child!" Eve smiled at her as she quickly ran toward her school.

When Caroline looked back at the tree, her fairy godmother and the carriage were gone!

Caroline walked into school with a big smile on her face. All her friends loved her costume, and she loved theirs.

She saw her friend Lily sitting alone by their classroom and sprinted to her.

"Lily, guess what! I met my fairy godmother and—"

When Caroline saw that Lily looked really sad, she stopped talking and sat down next to her. "What's wrong, Lily?"

"It's my costume. I don't like it."

Lily was supposed to be a fairy princess, but she wore one of her old dresses and a crown made of flowers. Caroline thought she looked really pretty though.

"I love your costume, Lily! It's so pretty!"

"You really think so?" Lily looked at her with a small smile.

"Yes! I think it's the best costume ever!" Caroline bumped their shoulders which made Lily laugh a little.

"Not as good as yours, though," her friend said.

"I think it's better because you look really, *really* pretty!"

Caroline made Lily smile bigger than ever! "Come on, let's go play!"

The two girls went to play with the rest of their friends until school started. The whole day was really fun for Caroline and she loved the different costumes that all her friends wore. Even her teacher wore a costume!

Caroline remembered what her grandma and Eve said about being kind. So when it came time for her teacher to say who won the costume contest, she was happy for who it would be.

"And the winner is... Caroline!" her teacher said and Caroline went up to the front of the class.

She smiled as her teacher gave her a small basket of chocolates and candy. "Can I say something?" she asked her teacher.

She said yes and Caroline looked at her class. "I want

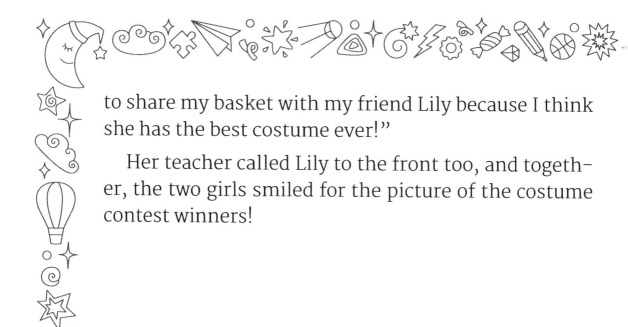

to share my basket with my friend Lily because I think she has the best costume ever!"

Her teacher called Lily to the front too, and together, the two girls smiled for the picture of the costume contest winners!

Thank you for buying our book!

If you find this storybook fun and useful, we would be very grateful if you could post a short review on Amazon! Your support does make a difference and we read every review personally.

If you would like to leave a review, just head on over to this book's Amazon page and click "Write a customer review."

Thank you for your support!